D1076643

the
perfect
world?

the perfect world?

Winners of
The Guardian/Piccadilly
writing competition for teenagers

Piccadilly Press • London

A catalogue record for this book is available
from the British Library

ISBN: 978 1 85340 981 3 (trade paperback)

1 3 5 7 9 10 8 6 4 2

Printed in the UK by CPI Bookmarque, Croydon, CR0 4TD
for the publishers Piccadilly Press Ltd,
5 Castle Road, London NW1 8PR
www.piccadillypress.co.uk

Cover photograph by Anne-Marie Weber/Getty Images
Cover design by Fielding Design

Mixed Sources
Product group from well-managed
forests and other controlled sources
www.fsc.org   Cert no. TT-COC-002227
© 1996 Forest Stewardship Council

Contents

Foreword

Jon Snow

My preconception was that, in the iPod internet age, teenage writers would have been diminished. I feared that texting and messaging, which so strip language of its descriptive power, would infect the teenage essay. I was wrong. This year's winners speak loudly and across the age range to a capacity for articulate and powerfully adjectival narrative that I think is as good as, if not better than, what my generation achieved in our pre-televisual, pre-computerised age.

This is class writing in any age and a huge encouragement for the future. Each of these winners has the potential to go much further. I'm now even tempted to wonder whether young people employ two different parts of the brain when they communicate – one for texting and messaging, the other for the long form, considered account. Maybe their more frequent and informal deployment of the written word, even in its truncated and often abused form, leads to a use of language that begins to transcend what my friends and I were capable of in our young teens. Or perhaps it speaks to the resilience of the human creative spirit, unbowed by the evolution of technology.

For me, judging these stories has been an uplifting voyage of discovery.

Aryan Utopia

Samuel Agbamu

Aryan Utopia

Summer 1955

All through the months of May and June, Mr von Klum had been rattling on about the closing years of the war, when the glorious army of the Reich had held off the invading allies in France, and how, about a year after that failed enemy invasion in Normandy, the allied forces surrendered to superior German forces in 1945.

Now, ten years after that, celebrations were to take place in Berlin and to be televised across the territories of the Reich, from Frank-Reich in the west to the Slavic countries in the east. Europe was enjoying a new era of plenty and peace under Nazi rule.

A pair of twins, Erika and Hans, having listened to Mr von Klum's patriotic rantings in history, were quite looking forward to watching the anniversary parade on the television set. When the day came, and the family was gathered around the television in the small, stuffy living room, the sun was blisteringly bright and the sky blue. Soon, Erika and Hans grew bored of the endless troops of soldiers in grey parading across the screen and went outside to play.

Their house was in a small logging village in the

3

country, surrounded by magnificent forest which offered the children near-infinite possibilities. Erika and Hans used to play wonderful games of hide and seek in the forest with a boy called Frank Klutz, but he and his family were moved to a Jewish containment settlement. People had always commented on the fact that two blond children shouldn't play with a dark-haired Jew. Hans had been told that the Jews were greedy and stole Germans' food and money, but Frank was such a nice boy, Hans wouldn't believe that he could do such a thing. It had to be said, though, that the German people had been enjoying an era of plenty as a result of the removal of the 'Jewish parasite' from mainstream society, or so Hans had been told.

Hans and Erika ran through the trees, imagining that they were soldiers, chasing fleeing Americans through the forests of Normandy. The leaf litter on the ground crunched under their feet, dried to a crisp under the hot sun. The children ran on deeper into the woods, to the rhythm of the crunching leaves, becoming slowly aware that they were no longer within the familiar play area of the forest.

Soon they stopped, in the shadow of a big tree, hands on their knees, panting through the exhaustion of the run. As their breath slowed down, they began to breathe through their noses. In doing so, they became aware of a strange smell. It was a smell of burning, but what was being burned the children were unable to ascertain. It was bitter and

4

made the children nauseous. They began to wander around the forest trying to identify the source of the smell, fearing that it was the smell of a forest fire that would put their father, a logger, out of a job. They followed the smell, deeper and deeper into the great forest. The air grew dusty and the smell grew stronger. The children came to a dusty road, which they were not previously aware of. How far must they have come to not recognise the roads?

They stepped on to the road, suddenly aware that they were lost. They couldn't even guess in which direction home lay. Hans bit his lip and scratched his head in exasperation, and pointed down the road.

'This way,' he said.

The sun, high in its daily arc, beat down on the children, tiring them with every step that they took in the dusty heat. They trudged on down the road, watching their feet kick up clouds of dirt.

After a while, Erika held up her hand, instantly stopping Hans and calling for silence. In the quiet, they heard a crow caw in a nearby tree, but there was also an underlying murmur of motors and machinery.

'The town!' exclaimed Erika excitedly. 'We are getting closer.'

The children resumed their journey, reinvigorated and excited at the prospect of nearing home. The noise got louder the further they went, until the children could no longer hear the sound of the trees whispering in the breeze.

It began to snow. Or rather, for a fleeting moment, the children thought that it had begun to snow, until logic took hold. Light flakes of white drifted from the blue, cloudless sky, save for a smudge of smoke, marring the stillness of the blue. The white flakes originated from the plume of dark smoke which the twins could see. They realised that the smell of burning must share a source with the smoke. The ash resulted in the air growing dusty and hazy, like looking through grimy glass lenses. Hans felt his throat dry out and he gagged, though whether it was because of the ash or the now overpowering smell, he did not know.

The undergrowth at the side of the road rustled, catching the attention of Erika and Hans. The sound was too large to have been produced by a squirrel or any such animal.

Tentatively, the children edged towards the place from which the sound had been emitted. Suddenly, the creature within the bush let out a cough, dry and weak.

'Hello?' called out Hans, shakily.

'Help,' replied the bush in a hoarse and quiet voice. The words were forced out with such effort that the twins believed that the occupant of the bush must be in tremendous pain or very ill.

Erika parted the bush and gasped, cupping both hands over her mouth.

Hans, peering into the bush, stumbled backwards and muttered, 'My God. What is it?'

The creature lay in the bush, curled up, as if it was protecting itself from an omnipresent threat. It was shivering, each shudder seeming to tear it apart. The sunlight, dappled by the bush, made the creature look like a starved leopard. Its skin, visible on its forearms and neck, was sallow and was stretched taut over bone. Its face was hidden by its arm, and its feet were cut and raw.

'Help,' said the creature.

Hans was a good person. In school, he was popular with the other students and teachers alike, due to his giving nature. Yet even his generosity wavered at the prospect of touching this thing.

Nevertheless, he reluctantly held his hand out to the creature in the bush. It took hold of Hans' hand with a feeble grip. Hans recoiled at the parchment-like touch of its hand, and heaved the creature out from the bush and set it down gently at the foot of a great tree, away from the road.

Here, in the coolness of the shade, the creature looked up into the eyes of Hans. Hans felt slightly sick at the face of the creature. The eyes were glazed over and bulging in the sockets, highly visible under the tight skin. The hair was reduced to stubble, violently shaved off, and the teeth, between thin, cracked lips, seemed comically too large for its mouth.

'Hans?' it said with a weak smile. Again it coughed,

shuddering violently as it did so.

'You know me?' asked Hans, puzzled and slightly fearful of the creature's knowledge.

The creature let out a single chuckle and immediately Hans realised that he had heard it before. The last time he had heard it, he was in the forest, not very far from where he stood now, playing hide and seek. Looking for Frank, he had heard this sound from behind a tree. 'Found you!' he had shouted as Frank emerged from his hiding place behind the tree, looking frustrated but happy.

'Frank?' said Hans, as if it was a suggestion.

Frank smiled a weak smile of recognition.

'What happened to you? What – how – I thought you had moved away.'

Frank's smile turned from that of a child to a dark one, on the face of someone who has suffered and seen all the cruel side of the world.

'We did,' he said. 'There.' He pointed to the road, down the side of which Hans and Erika were travelling. Erika was sitting on the side of the road, refusing to come any closer to Frank, disgusted at the way he looked. She lacked much of her brother's good will.

'But what happened to you? I mean . . .' Hans gestured at Frank with his hand.

Frank began to speak, before another coughing fit stopped him. When he spoke, it was in a barely audible whisper. 'Water. I need water. Please, I need water.'

Hans turned to the road where Erika sat.

'Erika! Go and get some water!'

'Where from?' she called as she picked herself up on to her feet, brushing down the dirt which had accumulated on her clothes.

'Frank said that his home is down the road there!' he replied pointing in the direction in which Frank had pointed. 'Try there!'

At once, Erika set off at a light jog down the road in the indicated direction.

'Wait!' Frank rasped, but it was far too quiet for Erika to hear.

'What's wrong?' asked Hans, concerned about his old friend's distress at Erika's departure.

'She shouldn't go down there. Shouldn't see. It's not right,' replied Frank, obviously struggling to get the words out.

'What? What shouldn't she see? What are you talking about?' Hans said, his voice raised slightly in panic.

'The camp.'

These two words alone seemed to visibly distress Frank, as Hans saw his face contort in the strain to hold in tears. He tried to speak, but instead of words, only tears came out. He sobbed weakly, with his face in his hands.

Hans crouched down next to Frank and put a hand on his shoulder.

'They took us in a truck. Said they were taking us

to another camp. I escaped. But Father, Joshua . . .'
Frank managed to get these words out, in between
tears, before a fresh fit of sobs rendered him
speechless once again. Hans remembered Joshua,
Frank's brother, although he never knew him well.
He was a young adult when Hans saw him last, too
old to play with them.

Suddenly, the memory of a film Hans had seen in
school was triggered in his mind.

The film showed a fat man in a black waistcoat
with a gaudy watch on a chain and a very large and
poorly made prosthetic nose, sitting on a pile of gold
in a beautifully furnished room exuding wealth with
every decoration. Meanwhile, out on the street, a
dirty father and son, dressed in rags, stood looking
into this rich miser's home, sad and longing. The son
turned to the father and said, 'Father, why must we
go wanting when this man has enough for a hundred
families?'

And Hans remembered the father's answer clearly.
'Because, son, the hand of the Jew is heavy on this
land.'

Then Hans realised where Frank and his family
had been taken. He realised what was being done to
Frank's people, the Jews. He realised, with grim
understanding, why this was being done. He heard
the answer of the father on the film again: 'The hand
of the Jew is heavy on this land.'

The Jews were being wiped out, so that the people

of the Reich could enjoy a perfect world. Frank had been taken to a camp to be killed.

Hans turned to Frank and said, grimly and in a raw voice, aged through the sudden burden on his soul, 'That ash.' He pointed to the sky, 'What is being burned?'

Frank sniggered callously. 'Jews.'

The sun was beginning to set, when Erika returned, but with no water. She was in hysterics, salty streaks down her face, giving away that she had been crying.

'Hans, what I saw . . . oh, dear Lord!'

Hans held up his hand – enough it said, but she continued anyway.

'I saw a cage. A cage made from wire. Ghosts in blue striped shirts and, oh, it was horrible, Hans, horrible, horrible, horrible.'

She wiped her streaming eyes with her sleeve, as if to erase the sight of the camp.

'But these ghosts, they were human. Humans in a cage like that! Who would do that! Who, Hans, who?'

She sat down next to Hans, against the tree, and put her head on his shoulder. She began to sob uncontrollably, shuddering in the chill evening breeze. Hans and Frank sat, silent and dazed by the cruelty of the world, waiting for the sun to rise and the darkness cease.

Life in the Shadows

Sally Bowell

Life in the Shadows

WAR HAS BEEN WON, ANNOUNCES REATH
Today Strickland Reath, our newly elected Prime Minister,
announced to an enraptured crowd that, 'The war has been
won. Perfection has been achieved.'

The ecstatic tumult which greeted his words reverberated
around the Central Conference Zone, a small tribute to
Reath's incredible work for the operation. Mrs Liza Pickering,
a senior governor for the SAP, the Society for the
Achievement of Perfection, announced in her speech that,
'Today will never be forgotten. I have been fighting for the
cause my entire life and I am so proud that I know I have
made a difference. Strickland Reath is my hero and I am so
happy to be here to witness this, the greatest of all days.'

It is widely accepted that the work of the SAP has had a
great effect on the outcome of the ongoing struggle for
Perfection. One spokesperson for the cause, addressing a
crowd of dwellers who were unable to obtain a pass for the
event, said, 'Without the SAP, no man, woman or child could
feel safe in their bed at night. Without the SAP, order would
not have been maintained amongst our rivals and without
the SAP, Perfection would not have been won. We owe all
that we have to their work.'

Andy threw the paper to one side. There was no more
he or anybody else could do now. He took a great

gulp of his tea only to discover it was stone cold. Light spilled into the kitchen from the far window but it was still not enough to wake him up fully. He missed the days when he could switch a light on by his bedside, his radio in the background pumping out music. Andy hated the endless dark, the rationed hour of electricity a day, the blandness of everything. Whatever happened to the junk food he used to love as a kid? Now his diet was so healthy that he had perfect skin, he had barely aged in the past five years and his teeth were glisteningly white. Beauty, youth and health were no longer something to be admired. They were now the only way to be.

Marina floated into the kitchen, her permanent smile fixed firmly in position and her doll cradled in her arms.

'Papa!' she called in her sweet singsong voice, making Andy shudder. 'Look at Sabrina, look how pretty her hair is: I plaited it!'

Andy gave a reluctant smile. He had to at least pretend to care. She skipped happily around the kitchen, pausing to sniff the flowers Liza had put on the windowsill. Marina was unperturbed by his lack of enthusiasm and ran back out of the kitchen, humming the tune from the new SAP advert. Andy sighed, crossed the kitchen, glad to be alone. He could not remember ever having been that happy when he was young. The majority of his memories from when he was ten consisted of him arguing with his brother about pretty much anything, his dad giving him a smack for swearing at the girl who lived next door and his mum and dad ignoring each other for a full twenty-four hours after a certain dispute. If he tried hard, he could just about recall sharing a Coke at Thorpe Park with Sandy Gardiner, the pretty girl in his class, and laughing for three minutes solid with his best friend Paddy. Those were the things that made a childhood.

Andy wondered what Marina would remember when she was his age. She was always bright, always bubbly, she did not even know the meaning of 'sad' – yet another thing they did not bother to teach children in school these days. When he had questioned Miss Donald, Marina's Year Four teacher, about this, the teacher had much to say, but none of it made any sense to Andy.

'Mr Pickering!' she had exclaimed, her lips tight, plastered with a terrible shade of pink lipstick. 'It is absolutely unnecessary to upset such a young child in this manner. I am sure you know the origins of Perfection, and I would just like to say that we support the SAP and the objectives of the order most strongly here at Chilworth Preparatory.'

Andy peered out of the clouded window to the high rising Central Zone, looking over his house, threatening everything he could call his own. Not that it was his house, not in the true sense of the word, not as it would have been twenty years ago.

The state owned his house. The state owned his sofa, his kitchen table, the cabinet he leaned on. They even owned his income, as they employed him. What could he call his own? His wife was an enthusiastic member of the SAP and his children were fed by their perfected nutrition, warped by their values and educated by their ridiculous Learning System. Everything, right down to the hair on his head – an implant to cover his natural baldness – was made and monitored by the order. Why did he endure that humiliation?

Andy stuck his hands into the washing up bowl, trying desperately to take his mind off the state of his life. The water was, as usual, cold and the dirt would not move.

So, this is Perfection? he thought. He knew he had work to do, but instead he stood looking out of the window at the lonely shed, floating in the wide expanse of lawn, enveloped by grey sky and suffocating under the thick mat of moss covering it.

Suddenly the doorbell rang, stirring Andy from his reverie. Remembering that Liza had left early for work, he trudged into the hall, reluctant to make polite conversation on the doorstep. Post littered the doormat, so Andy kicked it carelessly away. When the bell sounded again, Andy quickly unlocked the door and opened it. It was not any of the people who he had reasoned might call at this time of the morning. It was not the milkman or a neighbour or the postman. It was, instead, a very small, dishevelled woman, her dark brown hair scraped back off her head into a messy ponytail, her face creased, her eyes watery and her clothes, if not dirty, then tatty around the edges. She was staring at Andy and he felt colour rise up from the collar of his dressing gown and cover his face, slowly creeping up around his cheek, and finishing somewhere near his hairline. He was blushing; embarrassed to be seen with this woman, and for what reason? Here she stood, obviously desperate for his help, but something was holding him back. A tear eased its way down her cheek, falling softly on to the withered fur trim of her coat. The face of Reath flashed into his mind.

'Help those in need,' Reath had announced, 'but only those who follow the route to Perfection.'

'Can I help you?' Andy asked finally.

She smiled, her eyes suddenly bright and hungry with anticipation. 'I've been looking for you,' she whispered. 'Can I come inside?'

Andy nodded, now curious. He led her through into the kitchen, only just realising what he was doing. Luckily, Liza would not be home until late that evening. He gestured to a chair beside the table.

'I'd love to offer you a hot drink, but the hour's passed – no more electricity until tomorrow,' he said apologetically, somehow truly meaning it. His belly was warm, burning with an excitement and recklessness he had not felt in years. It was incredible,

19

he thought, how a dull life could be turned upside down in the space of a few minutes.

'It's OK,' the woman mumbled, just daring to raise her eyes to look at the first kind person she had met in weeks. 'What's your name?' she asked, her voice surprisingly gentle.

'Andy,' he replied and she nodded slowly.

He did not bother to mention his surname. It would be better if, for now anyway, she could make no connection between him and Liza who, being a senior governor for the SAP, was bound to scare her away.

'I'm Faye,' she said as she stood and made her way over to the window. 'I realise that you don't know me and I can hardly say that I know you, but, ever since that day I saw you in Piccadilly, when you turned away from the SAP billboard in disgust, I knew then that I was not alone. I managed to track you down.'

She leaned closer and closer into the glass until her nose was almost pressed against it. Her eyes glazed over as she concentrated on the small droplets of water running down. She raised her hand and let her fingertips brush against the glass, feeling the coldness seep through her skin. She shivered and turned back to Andy who sat watching her curiously.

'Look, I'm sorry to have bothered you and everything. I just . . . I need somebody to talk to and I thought it might be you. Will you listen?' Her eyes looked directly into his, questioningly. She was younger than Andy had first thought.

'I'm listening,' he said, a little apprehensively.

She looked relieved, but turned away from him again. 'I have been planning what to say for a long time now, but even so, it's almost impossible to know how to start. Maybe the beginning would be best, if you have the time.'

'Tell me everything,' he replied.

'I suppose it all started a year ago. I was living with my husband and my daughter Natalie. My husband and I were having marital problems, to say the least. Let's just say he found it hard to control his temper. Anyway, one day I'd had enough. I collected Natalie early from pre-school, saying we had a funeral to attend which I had forgotten to mention. Once we got home, I shoved as much as possible into a suitcase and we left. No, we ran. We caught a train to London, where I had imagined I could find work, and booked a hotel room for the night. Three weeks passed and I was no closer to finding a job. However, my husband managed to track me down through my credit card. I was stupid back then. So, Natalie and I had to run again. This time we chose Northumbria, as far as we could possibly get from London. This time, the card was cut.

'We settled into life there quite well for a month or so. Natty liked the fresh air and had the endless fields to enjoy. I found it relaxing, but there was no work. I was sick of scraping by on the dole, but what else was there to do? I was terrified of what my husband would do if he found us. I decided it would be better to be poor than dead.

'So, after a while we got used to checking the prices of bread and milk and we learned to love the damp in our rented flat. I still dreamed of finding work and getting us out of the situation we had found ourselves in. Imagine my delight, then, when I was approached one day. I was pinning a notice up on the library corkboard. *Handywoman to clean your house, manage your garden and keep the kids at bay.* A young man was standing behind me, surveying the board.

'As I turned around to leave he said, "I'm sure you're worth more than 'five pounds hourly'," he quoted, his nose upturned. "How about I offer you eight pounds an hour, without the snotty-nosed children and the wet dog to manage?"

'I was intrigued, even if I am embarrassed to say so now. You cannot understand how desperate I was: this was not the life I was used to.

'I turned up on the next Monday to see what he was talking about. It was pretty much as he had promised: a small office with ten employees. I filed records, answered phones and managed spread-sheets. It was nothing glamorous, but it was work. After a month or so, I began to wonder what these records were and who the person at the end of the line was and I set about finding the answers. Suspicion was dangerous in this organisation, as I soon found out.

The bruises from the beatings remained for several weeks, but the memory will stay imprinted on my mind forever. The attackers were employed by the company, as I soon realised. Threats began to litter my doorstep regularly and they ensured that I understood my place. I had no option but to stay. Mark was not a family man, as he had hinted. Instead, he was the leader of an organisation I had never heard of: the "R of N", otherwise known as the "Re-creation of Normality". I had inadvertently been signed into a life of criminal activity and I was trapped.

'Mark had told me there was another job I had to do – it would be easy, just slip in a house, bang, and the Senior Official of Health for the SAP would be dead. So I did it. But then the siren wailed and I knew what I had to do. I ran again. This time, however, I had to leave my darling Natalie behind.'

Faye shuddered, tears rolling down her tired face. She wiped them away hastily with her dirty hands. 'Slowly, one by one, the R of N is achieving its aim: to remove all opposition, or "pollutant factors" as it calls them. I need your help,' she concluded. 'I need you to protect me. The SAP discovered my involvement with the R of N and the punishment is . . .' She struggled to say it. '. . . hanging.'

Andy had never been a supporter of the reinstatement of capital punishment, but Liza had eagerly promoted the cause, insisting that anybody against the SAP was not perfect and therefore should be removed for the 'greater good'. Andy could barely begin to imagine Faye being killed for her involvement in this organisation, but he knew it was entirely likely. Suddenly he could feel her panic; he could understand her desperate plea.

'The shed, we can go there for now,' he said quickly, now lowering his voice, fully aware that Marina would still be playing with her dolls in just the next room. Adrenalin pumped the blood quickly around his body, his heart beating ferociously. 'Come on!'

Andy grabbed Faye's hand and dragged her over to the back door. He plucked the key off its hook, and eased it as quietly as possible into the keyhole. It clicked softly as he twisted it and he pressed his palm up against the wood, pushing it open.

It was drizzling slightly and black clouds loomed in the sky, promising more rain to come. Still holding hands, they ran down the side of the garden, taking care to duck down so as not to be seen over the fence. Shrubbery hid them from the view of the living room windows. They reached the shed and Faye pressed against the damp, rotting wall to hide herself from view. This door opened more easily and suddenly they were inside.

The shed was dark with only one miserable window allowing light to pass feebly through its cobweb-covered surface. It smelled of cut grass and sawdust. Nobody ever entered it as it only contained

DIY equipment, and, since the announcement that physical work undertaken by anybody but trained workers was dangerous, Liza had forbidden the use of most of this machinery. Andy settled down on the top of a paint pot and Faye sat on a sandbag. She smiled weakly at him. A loud click broke their silence. A light flashed from the corner of the shed, behind Faye, and suddenly he felt very uneasy.

'What was that?' she shouted, scrambling up from her seat and rushing to the opposite end of the shed, not taking her eyes off the little black box which they now saw hanging from the corner of the wall.

'I don't know!' Andy replied, terrified. If it was what he suspected, he and Faye were worse than dead. They were silent for a few further minutes, only the sound of heavy breathing to be heard from either of them.

Then Faye whispered, 'I have to go. I can't stay here. I think somebody is on to us. Let me out of the shed!' She was raising her voice now, desperate to leave. She scrabbled against the wood door, flakes of rotten wood falling off. 'Let me out!' she screamed. She turned to look at him, her eyes white with fear.

Andy could barely speak, so he held the key out to her. She snatched it off him, still searching his eyes for an explanation. She thought he had set her up.

She opened the door using the lower keyhole and it swung open, banging against the outer wall. Andy had barely turned his head to see her leave when she screamed. From the corner of his eye, he saw a black bag fall on her, enveloping her in darkness. She continued to scream, although now it was muffled.

As he had suspected might happen, Liza entered the shed, turning her nose up at the smell.

'Well done, Andy,' she said, attempting to brighten her voice in praise. 'I knew you would co-operate. The SAP have been looking for her for months and now you've finally tracked her down for us. You're a true supporter.' She smiled down at him.

Andy did not get up from the paint pot. He had failed. He had wanted to make a difference; to rebel against the SAP and their ridiculous vision. Instead, he had helped them.

He continued to sit, as Liza left the shed and joined her colleagues outside, laughing at the stupidity of the criminal and smiling at their own brilliance and their glittering vision of a perfect world.

Prohibited

Holly Burton

Prohibited

I live in a perfect world. Well, that's what *they* would say anyway. Personally, I don't think anyone or anything can be perfect except, maybe, God. If he actually exists. No one's proved if there is an omniscient being up there yet so I'm keeping my options open. Though I'm sure God would be the first person to say that their ideas of perfect are way off the mark. But if there is a God up there, I am praying so hard tonight that I don't get caught. Or killed.

I don't know why I'm writing this down. I mean, who else is going to read it, or for that matter, understand me? Even if I do die tonight, who is going to want to read the half-baked fantasies of a sixteen-year-old, illegal, homicidal maniac? Not that I agree that I'm murderous and crazy, but that's what they wrote on my record sheet. The one person in this freak of a planet that actually understands what I'm doing is probably going to join me in hell later anyway.

This makes me sound so pessimistic. Usually I'm quite a happy person – if someone shows me a glass of water, I'll always say it's half full – but the reality of what I'm about to do has hit me like a brick wall and I'm shaking and scared out of my mind and I really, really don't want to die.

I'm an illegal child. Illegal. Illicit. Unlawful. Prohibited. Banned. Whatever words they use it just means one thing. I should not exist.

Why should they decree whether I live or die? How can anyone tell me that my existence is worthless? But they do. Every day of my life. And I hate it. I hate them: the government and the scientists with all their stupid ideas about 'the perfect existence', and my school and all the kids that treat me like dirt . . .

This is turning into a bit of a rant. Think calm thoughts. Calm. Om.

Mandy does these weird yoga breathing exercises 'to get in touch with her inner being'. Personally I think it's a load of rubbish, all the charms and floating candles and stuff. I can't see why a few incense sticks are meant to help you 'find your true self' but it is strangely calming to sit and listen to the sound of your own breathing. We used to do it once a week. Sit, have herbal tea and a chat. Well, Mandy would chat, I listened. It was one of the new methods of mother-daughter bonding that the psychiatrist recommended. It doesn't work. She's not my mother. We don't bond.

Tom and Mandy expect me to call them 'Mum' and 'Dad'. I can't do that. It's . . . it just doesn't fit somehow. I used to, when I was about five, but not now. Not when I know . . . I'm getting ahead of myself. Actually half of this doesn't make any sense.

I just can't seem to be one of those people that explain things well. It's quite annoying actually. Trist can tell a joke, get the punchline and a laugh. Me? I stumble around and usually forget what I'm meant to be saying after the first sentence. I have been told I don't have 'natural social confidence', which isn't surprising considering I've also been told I'm useless my whole life. It doesn't take rocket science to figure the link.

I don't know who my real parents are. I know they were young, newly married. I think they were happy together. I sometimes imagine what we'd look like as a real family. We'd live together in a house far from the city and my mum would have my brown hair, I'd have my dad's brown eyes, and no one would ever find me or take me away from them.

Tristan hates his parents. Firstly because with a name like Tristan you have to be a rock star and, though he has the looks – blond mop of surfer's hair, blue eyes, slim body – he's also the biggest computer geek on the planet; and secondly because his attractive features come from a laboratory test tube.

At school they tell you the new system is better for everybody. A couple of hundred years ago, people were dying young at seventy. Now we can all live to be one hundred and fifty. People used to die of terrible genetic diseases. No one is born disabled now because they remove those genes. No one gets ill any more because modern medicine cures us before we're even born. The things they don't tell you about are all the children who went wrong. The test tubes that went faulty. It took thirteen attempts to make a perfect baby for Tristan's parents. His mum has coffee-coloured skin, black hair and green eyes and his dad is a redhead, but they chose Baby Type Seventeen: blond hair, blue eyes, twenty-twenty vision, perfect teeth and no genetic diseases, inclined to be clever, musical and handsome. If you give him a piano, Tristan can play Mozart perfectly – not that he likes Mozart, or the piano, but no one bothered asking him.

What about me? I was the first naturally conceived baby in two years to be discovered. They took me away from my parents and gave me to a couple unable to have children. I have a microchip in my skin monitoring my heart rate, hormone levels, blood pressure and temperature. I'm a walking, talking experiment available for junior biologists to examine and if I so much as sneeze I'm treated as if I have the plague.

We found this out by hacking into the lab computer system. Trist and me. I cried when I found out what they were doing to me. I cried so hard.

I was ten when I realised I was different and then Mandy told me I wasn't her child. We'd visit the scientists once a week for a routine check-up, because I could get ill and die when other people didn't.

Prohibited

When you get older you notice things. Like how strangers avoid you in the street, how children at school think you're weird. I started to ask questions. I didn't get answers. I saw psychiatrists, surgeons and specialists in sociology and science. My brain got poked and prodded and I sat test after test. That's when I got angry. They said I was psychologically disturbed because of my genetics and gave me tablets. I refused to take them. I made myself sick after I swallowed them. I hid the boxes. They drugged my food.

Tristan, my best friend, was my rock. He kept me sane. We made a pact, to find out what was really going on and when we did find out the truth, when I was sobbing my heart out on his bedroom floor, he hugged me and swore we'd run away together. Away from all this madness.

We stole a car and drove for miles and miles in the dark. Then he took a knife and cut out the chip from underneath my skin. The pain was unimaginable, indescribable. When I was six I broke my wrist but the pain was ten times more than that. The stitches were the worst because every needle prick felt like someone was stabbing me with a knife. He wrapped my arm in bandages and, when the tears were drying on my cheeks, he kissed me. He kissed me, and my heart is bursting now just thinking about it. Then we watched the night sky, hand in hand in a barn in the midst of a field of green, and I never knew there were so many stars in the sky or even in the whole universe.

We kept driving. On and on and on . . . the rain was falling slowly in the golden glow of a thousand streetlights. The drops of water clinging to my window, sliding down the cool glass to make tear-tracks in the middle of the frosty morning, froze into little stars that twinkled in the light of our torches, like the billions of distant galaxies up ahead.

One night we argued. I can't remember what about. He slammed the door and walked off into the darkness and I thought that he wouldn't come back. But he did. He said sorry and I said sorry. We both swore to love each other forever and fell asleep in each other's arms, parked in a back street near a council estate.

But we're here now. Outside a tall building, a typical warehouse, ignored by the people who pass it each day. But I know its secret.

This is where it all ends. This is when I finally find out the truth of who I am.

We'll hack into the government files and find where they've put my mum and dad and we'll rescue them. Then we'll run away to a house in the country and live away from all of it: my mum and dad, me and Trist. We'll get married and have proper children. Not test tube babies but real children, made from a part of me and a part of someone I love. And if I do grow old and grey and wrinkly I won't care, because it's the way I'm meant to be.

This is what I hope. This is what I'm praying for.

I don't know what will happen if we get caught. Probably be locked away in a mental hospital or perhaps I might simply 'disappear'. But I can't think about that. We will do it. We've got to.

I sit and watch the smog from the city turn to a red sunset; I watch the windows of the houses glow with the flickering light of a telescreen; I hear the sound of the traffic like dull thunder in the distance and I feel strangely calm. But, at this moment, this one quiet moment, I have never felt so alive.

Beneath the Surface

Nina Goodyear

Beneath the Surface

Kate

Kate gazed around the unfamiliar room, taking in the polished oak furnishings, the glass display cabinet and the oddly scattered pot plants wilting at the stems. In the corner of the room lay a large fish tank, home to three gloomy-looking goldfish which circled continuously around the tank. She supposed these details were intended to make her feel at home, but, on the contrary, the fixed stare of the largest goldfish only succeeded in unnerving her even more. She jumped as her thoughts were interrupted by the unexpected voice of Mr Douglas, breaking the silence.

'I can't help you, Kate, if you don't talk to me. I believe you wanted to speak about your older sister . . . Sarah?'

She picked at a loose thread in her jeans and nodded silently, subconsciously staring at the bald patch Mr Douglas had intended to conceal. As he followed her gaze, he flushed a shade of crimson, cleared his throat, and began once again.

'Your sister?'

Sitting up, Kate focused her attention for the first time this afternoon on the reason she had decided to search the Yellow Pages and had ended up there. Pleased that they were about to make progress, Mr

Douglas leaned back in his chair, crossed his legs and adopted his usual work position.

'My sister Sarah is everything I'm not,' Kate began abruptly. 'She was the most popular girl at school, captain of everything and all the boys loved her. I don't remember a time when she was ever alone.'

Mr Douglas smiled.

'I, however, never seemed to fit in anywhere and ended up spending most of my time alone. While she always had an endless string of boyfriends, I only had eyes for one person . . . one man.' She chewed her thumbnail, averting her eyes from Mr Douglas. 'The man she's married to now. Daniel and my sister were suited to each other, I suppose. He was the captain of the football team and was loved by everyone. But up until he married Sarah, I don't think he even knew my name. Anyway, now they're married, have a beautiful house in Chelsea and live the life of luxury. He is still ridiculously good-looking and earns more than I could dream of as a highflier in the city. Sarah is still as irritating as ever.'

Mr Douglas shifted in his chair and signalled for her to carry on.

'They don't have children now, but I'm imagining it's their next project . . . although it would spoil Sarah's figure . . .' She grinned and allowed herself a few moments to imagine her sister swelling to the size of an elephant.

Mr Douglas sat forward and spoke. 'And what about

you?' he said. 'Did you ever meet anyone else?'

Kate swallowed, hoping the prickly sensation creeping across her face would stop and prevent the tears from filling her eyes. There was no one else. At family dinner parties she would go alone as the token 'single' in the family. Sometimes she would make up boyfriends who 'cancelled at the last minute', but most of the time she just accepted that she was to be alone. In answer to Mr Douglas's question she shook her head and said, 'No . . . I have unrequitedly loved my sister's husband since long before they were married. But I'm beginning to realise that I've got to move on, and that's where I need your help, because he loves my sister. And as much as it pains me to say it, they're perfect together.'

Sarah

After sitting in the empty living room for almost an hour, Sarah finally accepted that he was not going to arrive. Refilling her glass with yet another helping of red wine, she got up and stalked towards the kitchen. The candles were lit, the table was laid and the room looked beautiful. If things had been different, she would have smiled triumphantly at her 'romantic-dinner-effort', but instead she swore and ran to the oven which was beginning to emit burning smells. Grabbing the oven gloves, she plunged her hands into the oven and pulled out a blackened casserole, slopping some of the remnants on to her new outfit in her haste. Now fuming, Sarah grabbed the kitchen phone and punched in her husband's number. Expecting the answer phone (like the other three times she had tried ringing him that night), she was surprised to hear his voice on the other end of the line.

'Hiya,' he said in his usual nonchalant manner, 'I'm sorry I'm running late – last-minute meeting. I was going to call you but . . . you know . . . ' He let his sentence trail off into the icy silence that followed.

Sarah swallowed, trying not to explode. 'No, Dan, I don't know why you didn't call me. It would've been nice to know you weren't coming home, then I wouldn't have bothered making us dinner. Not that we can eat it now anyway.'

Daniel did not reply for some time, the awkward silence growing more and more awkward. Then Sarah noticed talking in the background; her husband's voice and another, unfamiliar one. Finally he replied, sounding irritated.

'Look, I don't see what all the fuss is about – we can have dinner any night. I have a commitment to my job and if you can't —'

'You're not at work, are you?' Sarah interrupted, a lump building in her throat. As soon as she'd said it, she regretted challenging him. For a long time she had been suspicious of his continual late nights, but she'd never really believed he would cheat on her.

This wasn't her talking . . . When had she become so paranoid? When she and Daniel were younger, they had been the envy of everybody. She had been closer to him than she had ever been to anybody . . . but things were different now. They hardly talked and, when they did, Daniel would often snap at her or walk away. The harder she tried to put things right between them, the worse things seem to get. When did it get so bad?

'I'm sorry . . . I – I didn't mean it,' she stuttered, a hint of desperation in her voice. 'Daniel?'

There was a long pause. The kitchen fell so silent Sarah could hear the monotone tick of the clock in the background.

'You're pathetic,' he said finally, and immediately tears welled in Sarah's eyes.

'Please come home,' she pleaded. And then the call ended. The electronic beep filled the ever-growing gap between them. Placing the phone back on to the receiver with a trembling hand, she blew out the candles and walked numbly up the stairs.

Kate

Sitting now in a warm and comforting bubble bath, Kate reflected on her conversation with Mr Douglas earlier that day. For some reason, she had been able to open up and confide in a complete stranger the secrets she had never been able to tell anyone. For instance, as far as she knew, nobody realised how she felt about Daniel and nobody realised quite how envious she was of her sister. Ever since they were children, Kate had always been in her sister's shadow, shunted into second place wherever Sarah was concerned. And her parents didn't help. When Sarah came home with a certificate for this or one hundred per cent in that, and she would arrive with nothing, her parents would ask, 'Why can't you be more like Sarah?'

And often she wondered that herself. How can some people end up with everything and others nothing? For a start, Sarah's loaded. Although she gave up work after she married, she still gets enough from Daniel to ensure she never leaves the house in anything less than designer clothes. Sarah has the job, the man, the house . . . the life. How is that fair?

And what do I have? she thought to herself bitterly. I live in a small flat, I pay rent, I've worked in the same office ever since I left university and I'm single. Great. Thoroughly depressed by her gloomy contemplations, she clambered out of the bath, wrapped a towel around herself, and headed straight for bed.

Sarah

By ten o'clock in the morning, Adam Douglas had decided that it was going to be a bad day. It had started at six-thirty, when his alarm clock had failed to wake him up, and had continued throughout his

44

journey to work. Before entering the office he had managed to leave the house without his wallet, tear his suit jacket on a car door and lose his keys for the second time that day. And to top it all, he was beginning to notice the symptoms of a rather nasty migraine. Now, sitting in front of an ever-growing mountain of paperwork and folders, he had managed to knock over his cup of coffee, staining his white shirt and all of the papers in front of him. Jumping up, he let out a flourish of bad language (enough to shock the goldfish circling in the tank beside him) and began to frantically mop up the mess with his tie.

'Marvellous,' he muttered, 'just what I need.'

Still fuming, he snatched the phone from his desk as soon as it started to ring and barked down the line, 'Adam Douglas!' On the other end of the phone, the receptionist muttered her apologies for calling at what seemed to be a bad time.

'Mr Douglas,' she began, 'there's someone here who would like to see you – a Mrs Sarah White. She's been coming to see Louise Harris for some time, but Louise is off sick today. I hope you don't mind, but I said I would ask if you would agree to see her instead . . . She seemed quite desperate to see somebody. I put her file on your desk earlier this morning, just in case.'

Groaning, Adam gazed down to look at the file in front of him, which bore the brunt of the black coffee stain. Sure enough, the name on the front read Sarah White. Kicking himself for being such an idiot, he began wiping at the file, trying to undo the damage.

Still on the line the receptionist coughed, anxiously awaiting a reply.

'I'm sorry . . . ' he mumbled, holding the phone awkwardly to his ear with his shoulder as he continued to scrub. 'I'm just having one of those days where I feel I need reminding why I do this job.'

The receptionist smiled and parroted, 'Therapy is a very rewarding job.' It was a standing joke between them. She grinned then continued, 'So can I tell Mrs White you'll see her?'

Adam reluctantly agreed, then put down the phone and quickly skimmed through his unexpected client's file.

'Married, lives locally . . . ' he read aloud, pausing at the next line. 'Often very depressed . . . the cause being her husband whose late nights are an area that causes her concern. In summary – has a deteriorating relationship with her husband who fails to see anything is wrong . . .' Slipping off his glasses, he folded the papers back into the file and placed it back on to his desk. 'Sounds like we should get both of them in here,' he muttered, before calling out for the lady to come in.

Sarah White was nothing like he had imagined her to be. She was tall, with an air of grace and (Adam couldn't help noticing) she was very attractive. What surprised him the most about Sarah was the fact that she seemed so confident, unlike his usual clients. He would probably describe the classic client as quiet, introverted and severely lacking in self confidence – very much like the lady he had seen the day before. A little taken back, he jumped to his feet and warmly shook her hand as she seated herself in the chair next to him.

'I'm Adam Douglas,' he began, feeling a little tongue-tied. 'I understand you've been seeing Louise for some time?'

She nodded, her gaze passing over the black coffee stain across his tie and shirt disapprovingly.

Subconsciously, he rubbed his hand across it, once again flushing crimson.

'I started seeing Louise a few months after I got married,' she began, finally making eye contact. 'It sounds pathetic, I know, but I needed someone I could talk to about my worries . . . I've been seeing her when I needed ever since.' She stopped abruptly and looked down to the floor, as though she had admitted something embarrassing. Adam picked up on this at once.

'You seem ashamed about this, Sarah,' he said. 'There is nothing wrong with admitting you needed help.'

Once again, Sarah avoided eye contact. She began to gaze around the room, focusing on the wilted pot plants much in need of some TLC.

'It's just . . .' she said, 'I'm not the kind of person who goes to therapy. All my family and friends know me as the confident, happy Sarah who has no problems to worry her. And I suppose I shouldn't really . . . but the truth is, I do. I worry about my husband . . . the man who used to idolise me . . . who loved me like nobody else ever could. And now he can't even stay in the same room as me. We constantly fight . . . and he didn't come home last night.' She began rummaging around her handbag until she found a tissue to dab her eyes. 'If anyone saw me like this,' she continued wiping her nose, 'they wouldn't believe it was me!' She forced a laugh and again looked to the floor.

Adam remained silent, encouraging Sarah to keep talking. When she didn't proceed, he prompted her with a question. 'Why is it so important for you to keep up this false appearance? Surely you are only deceiving yourself?'

It didn't take long for her to answer. She shook her head. 'No . . . it's partly because of my sister. She thinks of me as this wonderful role model, living this perfect life . . . which I'm not. She doesn't know how unhappy I am . . . ' She let her sentence trail off. 'And you know what the biggest secret is?'

Adam shook his head, a sudden understanding dawning on him at the mention of a sister.

'She doesn't know how much I envy her.' After this confession, Sarah fell silent.

Glancing at her, Adam rubbed a hand across his chin, and sighed inwardly. Only now did he realise who this lady was and why her story had seemed so familiar. Knowing better than to blurt out this new-found link, however comforting it might have been, Adam sat for the rest of the consultation, nodding and listening to Sarah. While she spoke about her sister's 'independent and carefree' life in comparison to hers, which was 'paranoid and dull', Adam resisted with difficulty the urge to intervene and put his client straight.

When the hour drew to a close, Sarah got up, thanked Adam and returned home to a cold and empty house. She fussed about the rooms, finding unnecessary errands to fill the time, and checked the clock every few minutes for her husband's long-awaited return.

Meanwhile, Kate sat at her office desk, drowning under a heap of paperwork, and thought of her sister. She wondered whether Sarah might be out shopping or at an outrageously expensive spa or, better still, could Daniel have nipped home unexpectedly and whisked her off to a surprise lunch? All equally likely, Kate thought to herself with a smile.

As Sarah prepared a meal she hoped she wouldn't have to eat alone, she suddenly thought of Kate. Speaking to the therapist earlier had brought to light thoughts she hadn't even admitted to herself. She had never really appreciated how strong her feelings towards her sister were, nor how much she hated herself for being the cause of their broken relationship. She had been selfish, wrapped up in her new life. They had once been so close.

But it doesn't have to be this way, Sarah thought to herself, a decision finally dawning upon her as though it was the most obvious of things. Knowing for the first time in years that what she was doing was right, she picked up the phone, hesitated briefly, then dialled the number she had never forgotten.

Five O'Clock Last Thursday

James Hardman

Five O'Clock Last Thursday

A perfect world can mean many things to many different people. To some, it can mean intense material wealth, with every desire, every whim catered to in the unending search for satisfaction. For others, it can mean liberation from material needs: an enlightened world in which everyone is equal and has everything that they need to make them truly happy.

One man's own perfect world came to an end, quite suddenly, at five o'clock last Thursday.

Winter. The silent, icy passion of snow crystals covered the groaning city in a blanket of white. From the air, it resembled a blank sea, dotted only with the occasional dark islet which the snowflakes had not yet touched. In the depths of this freezing ocean, a thousand stories took place, all interlinked by an invisible web of cause and effect. On a street to the north, the still-warm body of a young girl lay cooling in a pool of frozen blood. To the south, a shop was broken into, the thieves looking for anything that they could sell and get away with. Westwards, in the rundown housing estate, a group of young criminals, brought together by their hatred for society, schemed and plotted and fought amongst themselves for the drugs and money that they believed could make their lives a little less dreadful.

And to the east, in a quiet suburb on the edge of town, a man pulled up on his drive in his old, faithful Ford transit van. Getting out of the car, an observer would have noticed that he was of average height and medium build, with a full crop of dark hair that was rebelliously going grey at the roots. An observer did notice that his face was full and happy, with deep laughter lines crinkling the skin around his sparkling, cobalt-blue eyes as he chuckled at the joke his son, getting out of the van just behind him, had told. The watcher's hidden eyes followed the father and son, both wearing matching bottle-green hoodies, as they locked up the vehicle and then walked up to the front door, leaving twin footprints in the virgin snow behind them.

Into the house the man and his son went, in through the open doorway into a passageway that smelled of home. Pictures of places the family had been on holiday hung from the walls: here, a watercolour of that town they visited in the Loire; there, some caricatures drawn by a street artist in Rome. Memories of sun and sea and happiness displayed to all who passed through. Past the ancient grandfather clock and on into the kitchen, guided by the sweet aroma of home cooking that hung in the air like a bright trail, promising relief from hunger.

The man's wife glanced up from the stove as her

husband and eldest son came in. He came over to her and they embraced, their love still as strong as iron after eighteen long years of marriage. The son sat down at the table next to his younger brother, finishing off the holiday work that he had been set. Tonight, they needed to eat early: to catch the plane to Sydney, they would have to set off within the hour.

Suddenly, a noise that would not only have wakened the dead, but made them dance too, echoed around the cosy confines of the kitchen. Everyone jumped, looking for the source. Within moments, however, it had come bounding into the room, its four padded paws pounding on the ground, jumping up and down like a demented rabbit.

Their pet Alsatian satisfied and supper ready, the youngest son put away his maths and the rest of them took their places around the long oak table in the centre of the room. The man felt utterly content. He had a loving family, a beautiful home, a job which he loved and would soon be able to share with his son. He had a perfect life.

The grandfather clock in the hallway struck five.

The man had just put the first mouthful of steaming hot beef stew – his favourite – into his mouth when the door was burst open by an armed gunman dressed all in black, two more hot on his heels. With an almighty bark, the dog launched himself at the first intruder, but mid-leap he was mown down by a dozen bullets from the others. The man jumped up. Deafened by the gunshots that had exploded only three feet from where he was sitting, he didn't hear the yells of the gunmen. He too flew at them, enraged by the cruel murder of his pet, but quickly he fell to earth. Three shots in the stomach. Two in the chest. One to the head.

To the man, it seemed that it had all suddenly gone quiet, as if someone had turned the volume down on a TV. Out of the corner of his darkening eyes, he saw his wife and family, screaming and kicking in grief and terror, being dragged away. His blood spread across the floor his wife had tried so hard to keep clean, intermingling with that of his dog. His vision slowly faded. Breathing became harder, until eventually it did not seem worth the effort. Consciousness collapsed. His last fleeting thought was to wonder what had he done to deserve this.

POLICE FILE 8264/1b
Statement given by: Detective Inspector David Johns

At 16.27 several squad cars had been despatched to deal with a break-in in the commercial district downtown. As they chased the thieves, two of our officers broke off pursuit to deal with a serious incident. According to witnesses from a nearby building, a young schoolgirl, walking alone on her way home, was approached by two tall men. The officers were unable to obtain descriptions since their faces were obscured by hoods. As the men came close, one of them pulled out a six-to-eight-inch blade and, whilst his accomplice grabbed hold of the girl, severed her carotid artery. The men then exited the scene in a white Ford transit van and drove away, heading eastwards. The witnesses from the building crowded round the body, at which point officers PC Jones and PC Sanders arrived.

Using their own initiative, the two constables set off in the same direction as the van and, due to the lack of traffic, quickly caught it up. They followed the van over to the eastern suburbs and, concealed in a neighbour's garden, watched the two men enter their house. Once confirming them as the murderers, they called for an armed response team.

When this team arrived they forced their way into the house and were viciously attacked by the family's large dog. Unfortunately, they were forced to terminate it for their own safety. One of the suspects then rushed at the officers, ignoring their commands to get down on the floor. The armed response team had no choice but to stop him with all necessary force.

Upon questioning, the deceased's son told us the whole story. His father was the man we had been searching for – the one known in the press as 'the Ripper'. He was a contract killer who specialised in brutal, shocking murders. This particular killing was done on behalf of a local drugs lord; the victim was the daughter of the city's anti-vice commissioner. This was the first time that his son had joined him, but the family had always known what he did. The steady income allowed them to live quite well – making hell for others allowed them paradise.

Heaven's Perfection

Christy Ku

Heaven's Perfection

I rolled over, sighing. I didn't want to get up: my bed was so warm, and soft like a cloud. I opened one eye. I sat up bolt upright, bewildered. I *was* on a cloud. I slapped my face hard. Obviously, it was a dream. Then the memories flooded back, snaring my mind, twisting my sanity. Images flashed in my head, so terrible, so painful. I shook with fear as the memories unfolded.

'It's all right, it's all right,' called a low, gentle voice. 'Welcome to heaven. You're at the reception. I'm God.'

An invisible hand was on my forehead and the painful memories were gone. I began to calm down.

'What?' I said. I was wearing a long white robe and *had feathery wings?* How embarrassing – I must look like a two-year-old dressing up as a fairy.

'Sorry, you didn't stand a chance of surviving. Just sign in here. No terms or conditions apply,' said the voice.

Bewildered, I wrote down my name in a thick book with a feathered quill pen. I was taken through an archway on a drifting cloud. I gasped. I saw beautiful white buildings, made from marble and moonstone, towering above me. Roses and other flowers of wonderful beauty entwined around pillars, framed by angelic rays of golden light. A relaxing scent of lavender and vanilla floated on the gentle cool breeze. A soft low flute echoed around in the lush green valley, the sound emptying my mind of troubles. The city was a perfect combination of man and nature.

'Hello, are you new?'

I spun around and gazed at the speaker. She had a heart-shaped face, with light golden hair floating in the breeze. Her long white robe was embroidered with a thousand buttercups. I was stunned by her beauty. I became self conscious, thinking about my thin black hair and pale skin. She seemed to read my mind and gave me a mirror. I looked into it and was amazed. My dark hair was de-frizzed, flowing down to my waist. My fair skin was smooth and unblemished.

'I was like you. I remember it like it was an hour ago. I'm Claire. Don't let my mind-reading scare you. You get it when you've been dead for four hundred years.' She smiled. 'What's your name?'

I swallowed. I had a weird name.

'Jin—'

I was cut short as the other angel quickly put her hand to my mouth.

'Don't say that word. It has terrible results,' she muttered. She smiled again and repeated more loudly, 'I'm Claire. Do you want to see seventh heaven? It's really posh.'

A week later, I was relaxing contentedly in a café, drinking a glass of iced orange juice with Claire.

'How did you die?' I asked timidly. Her calm smile dropped.

'I . . . I don't remember . . . I mean – it was four hundred years ago,' she stuttered. 'Do you remember?'

My mind was blank. My death was only a week ago. Claire was about to change the subject when I ran. I had put the same questions to other angels and had got the same reply. I ran on and on to the Head Office. I needed an answer. With the door flying open, I crashed into the office. No one was there. I glanced around and saw a door labelled *The Forbidden Room*. Taking a deep breath, I entered.

It was dark grey inside. Thousands of voices whispered eerily, glass jars of black swirling smoke rattled on the shelves.

'Here I am. I'm your memory. Release me. Release us all,' a voice rasped, like sandpaper against gravel. 'See what happened.'

I grabbed the jar with my name on it. There was a delighted laugh as I opened it. The laugh turned into a scream as the acidic smoke swamped into my eyes.

I was walking home from school with friends after a detention. We were late, so I decided we should take a shortcut. My friends were uneasy, but they were desperate. My shortcut was across a railway line. The train should have gone to the station ten minutes earlier. I slipped through the fence and leaped over the electric part on to the middle of the track. I turned to wave them across. They were frozen to the spot with wide eyes. One screamed and pointed. When I looked, a train was coming, sickeningly fast. I heard a screech of brakes and the train was on me, a horrific thud to my stomach. I was dragged under the wheels, screaming in agony. Black and white flashes in front of my eyes. I felt my body being torn – and I blacked out.

I gasped and clutched a nearby shelf as I came back to reality. I felt waves of home sickness crash over me. I would not see them for many, many years. My mum, dad and friends must be going mad at my death, especially little Hannah. My poor sister, she was only five. She wouldn't understand a thing. My life in heaven was a misery. My heart longed to leave my soul and be on Earth. I began to hate this perfect world. Everything was pristine. I missed getting into trouble, seeing imperfect people. My heart ached to be back on Earth.

'Release us. Release us and we'll release you.' All the voices were chanting the same message, over and over. I knew what to do. I ran to the door and said one word. My name.

'Jinx.'

The bottles burst open, the glass showering the room like a sudden downpour. The smoke swept me away. I fell through the normally solid clouds, down to Earth. I was falling, falling, a bird with no wings, crying for help . . .

* * *

I opened my eyes. It was pitch black. It had all been a dream, a nightmare. Relief was intoxicating. I sighed and sat up. I had barely lifted my head when it hit something soft. I flopped back down again. I tried to move, but my body wouldn't respond. The air was starting to get hot. It was so dark, I didn't know whether I had my eyes opened or closed. I could smell blood. The truth struck me like a thunderbolt. I had come back from heaven to my body. If I had been hit by a train . . . I felt sick. My body was in several parts, but I was alive. Buried alive! I used my arm to pound the sides, clawing at the velvet inside of the coffin, a cold flood of desperation rushing into my head. I pounded the ceiling, ignoring the growing pain in my head. An iron fist was clenching my throat. I gaped and gave a final punch.

I felt a familiar softness and warmth. I was on a cloud again. A dove was looking at me.

'Welcome back to heaven. You're only supposed to die once.' The voice came from the dove, but it didn't open its beak. 'It seems like you've found out that no world is perfect. Even in the purest of places, there always will be darkness. Never mind; all the memories have been taken back to the Forbidden Room. There's no harm done, child. Your name is a spell, but it won't matter unless you come into my office and say the name. Now, perhaps . . . some work. Come, my daughter – I have the perfect task for you.'

Twenty years later

Hannah shut the door and sat down in front of her dressing table mirror. She was eager to test out a superstition. She was alone and it was a dark night. The young woman lit a candle and held it in her hands. The flickering light sent long shadows which danced upon the black walls. Holding the candle under her face, she looked into the mirror. According to the legend, you would see your guardian angel.

Hannah stared. In the mirror, she could only see herself. Then a winged figure stepped behind her. Hannah looked around shakily. No one was there. She turned back into the mirror and looked at the angel's face. Hannah gasped. The angel was Jinx.

Too Good To Be True

Emily Lynch

Too Good To Be True

It was perfect. Just then, just at that precise second. He had everything he ever wanted right in front of him. He could never have imagined having this amount of happiness. He had everything he had ever dreamed of: a beautiful wife and, very soon, a wonderful new baby. He felt as if he couldn't even move, everything had just taken him over. He held on to his wife's hand as the baby's head crowned, and he kept hold of it as if he was too scared to let go, in case all this turned out to be a dream and this feeling of actual happiness would disappear. It all seemed too good to be true.

In a second, his son was out. A rush of happiness washed over him. He was here, he was finally here!

Suddenly machines started buzzing and Jeremy was snapped back to reality. This wasn't right, this wasn't meant to happen. Doctors and nurses rushed over, shoving Jeremy out of the way. He was too shocked to move. He stared down at his wife, unable even to breathe. He was led out of the room by one of the nurses, but his eyes were still fixed firmly on his wife.

They lowered her head down and started attaching all kinds of machines to her. Jeremy was out of the room now, but in his head he could still hear the sounds of the machines shrieking so loudly. He felt as if his heart had just been ripped out of his chest and torn apart. He broke down on the floor and his shoulders shook uncontrollably. The tears wouldn't stop. He had had happiness for just that second, and it was so quickly ripped away from him that he hadn't even had enough time to take it in, take in what he had waited his whole life for. He couldn't lose her, he wouldn't let her die. He felt so helpless. He stared through the glass at his wife, wishing she would open her eyes and everything would be just how they had planned it. He wished he could turn back time, so that he could tell her she had made him the happiest man in the world, and without her he was nothing.

He sat there for over an hour. The fear was just too much for him. He couldn't seem to take his eyes off the door. He kept telling himself that the next person to walk out would be the nurse, telling him that his wife was fine. He kept wishing he would still live happily ever after.

His heart stopped. The nurse walked over to him, and paused. 'I'm so sorry, Mr Thomas,' she said. 'The childbirth put too much strain on your wife's heart. It was all too much for her body to take. It was so unexpected – there was nothing we could do. I'm so sorry.'

His whole world felt as if was crashing down around him. His body seemed to shut down. He couldn't take in what the nurse was saying, his brain was rejecting the information because it didn't want to hear it. He felt no emotion.

'Would you like to see her, say your final goodbyes?'

Suddenly, it hit him. The word 'final' kept bellowing in his head. Final? When he realised that this was going to be the last time he saw her, he felt his heart break inside him. The nurse took his hand and led him through the double doors to the delivery room. He took his wife's cold limp hand in his.

'I love you; you h-have made me,' he stuttered, wiping his face on the back of his sleeve, 'the happiest man in the world, Alice Thomas, you know that? I love you, and I always will.'

He was led outside by one of the nurses. His entire body was numb. He felt like he couldn't even cry anymore. His eyes were so swollen from crying that he could hardly see where he was going.

'Do you have any family you want me to call?' asked the nurse, helping him to sit down on to one of the nearby chairs.

He couldn't think about that right now, he didn't want anyone near him; he needed to be alone. He looked up at the nurse, eyes still puffy and bloodshot, but no words seemed able to come out. He just needed to be alone, why did no one seem to understand? The nurse brought him through to the bereavement room and said she was going to call his father. But he didn't want his dad there, he didn't want anyone there.

The next morning, he woke and his whole body was stiff. He had hardly slept a wink. He saw his dad sitting in the corner, talking on his mobile.

'Yes, right, OK. He's just waking up now so I'd better be going. I'll call you later with news of the baby. Yep, bye.' He put his phone away and walked over to his son.

'Son, I'm so sorry. I know there's nothing I can do to make things any better, but I will be here for you no matter what, Jez, OK? We all will.' He hugged his son for what seemed like hours. 'Shall we go and see him, Jez? I want to meet my first grandchild,' he said, trying to force out a smile.

They walked into the nursery and that new baby smell surrounded them. Jeremy's dad asked where 'baby boy Thomas' was. Jeremy felt, in a way, that he didn't want a son right now. He wanted to grieve for his wife alone, he didn't want the strain of a baby hanging over him.

He stared at this baby, and all he could see was Alice. He had her nose, her big brown eyes and her jet black hair. Jeremy's body was overcome with emotion.

'Decided what you're going to call him yet, Jez?' his father asked.

Jeremy hadn't thought about any of this yet. Even

he and Alice hadn't decided on a name. They had both had ideas, but they hadn't actually settled on a definite one. Alice's favourite name, which she had liked since she was little, was Daniel. She had liked the way Daniel and Thomas sounded together.

Jeremy had never liked it, he said it was too common, and he would be about the seventh Daniel in his class.

'Daniel,' he replied.

The next day, they were allowed to take him home.

Jeremy still felt he couldn't face even looking at Daniel, as every time he saw him he saw Alice.

His father was holding the baby in his arms, blowing raspberries on his chest. 'Can you hold him for one second? I need to go and talk to the nurse outside,' he said, holding Daniel out to Jeremy.

Jeremy stared at his father, then stared at the baby, then back at his father and back at the baby. He couldn't even hold his own son. He lay down on the bed and shut his eyes. He wanted to go sleep and never wake up.

Later that afternoon, they took Daniel home. When Jeremy's weak fingers opened the door, Alice's smell surrounded them. He saw one of Alice's jumpers hanging over the banister and a cup of cold coffee she hadn't had time to finish before they left for the hospital. Suddenly that feeling rushed over him again. The feeling he got when he saw the nurse and the first time he saw Daniel. That feeling of complete heartache. He couldn't deal with any of this.

'I'll take Dan upstairs and then make us both some tea, OK, Jez?' his father said, already heading up the stairs.

That night, Jeremy lay there in the darkness, unable to sleep, even though his eyes were so heavy he felt as if they were practically shut already. The thought of everything made him sick. He kept thinking of how Alice would have coped if she was in this situation, and if he had died instead. She would have never given Daniel any less care because of it.

Jeremy got up and slowly walked into Daniel's nursery. He picked him up and cradled him in his arms. From then on, he swore to himself, he would always be there for his son, no matter what.

The Wrong Turn

Francesca Scott

The Wrong Turn

As he entered the station, Sam Bennet passed the duty officer at the front desk.

'Interview Room Four?' he asked.

'Yeah, the usual,' said the officer, without looking up from his magazine.

Turning the corner and starting to walk down the dingy corridor, Sam wondered how he had ended up like this. His life had changed completely in the past few months, and, walking by the familiar doors and noticeboards, Sam tried to contemplate where it all began. Perhaps it was that cold winter's night, back in December . . .

Sophie heard the front door slam and ran out into the hallway.

'Daddy's home!' she shrieked, jumping into her father's arms before he'd had a chance to take off his wet coat.

On hearing the noise, Daisy, the old golden labrador, padded out to greet Sam. Panting and wagging her tail excitedly, she jumped up, demanding his attention. After stroking the dog, Sam tickled Sophie, who squealed with delight as he carried her into the kitchen. His wife Helen was making pasta for dinner, but stopped stirring for a moment to give Sam a kiss on the cheek.

Helen was of medium height, slim, with mousy brown hair, hazel eyes and a face which lit up when she smiled. She had been a housewife for seven years, since the birth of their son Josh and most recently four-year-old Sophie. The routine of everyday chores and housework was tedious, but having children was rewarding, and, on the rare occasions when things became too much for Helen, she could always count on her loving husband to help her cope. She had first been attracted to Sam's sense of humour and his warm, exuberant personality, and, although he had grown calmer and plumper with age and his dark hair was showing signs of grey, nine years on they were still happily married.

'How was your day?' she asked.

'Work was fine, nothing out of the ordinary,' replied Sam in a rather gloomy tone. 'Anyway, let's not talk about that now. Who wants to play a game before dinner?'

Josh and Sophie eagerly ran off to fetch the battered Twister set, and they played several games with Sam before collapsing in fits of giggles on the carpet. After Daisy had been fed, Helen served their meal on the table – penne pasta with tomato sauce. While they were eating, Josh decided that this was the perfect moment to ask for the toy that he wanted. Having described in great detail his brilliant result in a recent maths test, he asked with a glint in his eye, 'By the way, could I have the new Spider-Man action set for Christmas? Everyone else in my class is getting one.'

This prompted Sophie to enquire about the arrival of her Barbie. Their parents looked at one other across the table.

'We'll see,' answered Sam.

'Please!' begged Josh.

'Both of you will have to wait and see what Father Christmas brings this year,' said Helen firmly. 'But he will only come if you're good.'

Once the children had gone to bed, Helen enquired, 'Is there any news on that Christmas bonus of yours? The kids want even more expensive toys this year, and we could really use a little extra cash.' She spoke gently, not wanting to upset Sam, who was very sensitive about financial matters.

He sighed. 'Yes, the Chief told us today, and it's next to nothing. After all my work, it's not even close to what we had hoped! The worst part is that Jack got at least four times my bonus, and he's always late and missing his deadlines. He seems one step ahead of me in almost everything. I don't know how he does it.'

Helen tried not to show her disappointment, knowing she needed to stay supportive. She was sure it wasn't Sam's fault and there was no point in fretting.

'Well, we'll have to cut down on spending for a while – there isn't much else we can do. I suppose I could look into a part-time teaching job somewhere local —'

She was cut off quickly as Sam interrupted her.

'No, I won't let that happen. It's up to me to sort this out; I'll think of something. Don't worry.' Changing the conversation to something light-hearted, he began to clear up the dishes.

Later that night, lying in bed and trying to sleep, Sam couldn't stop thinking of money. He pretended that it didn't bother him, but he often found himself envying Jack, a fellow police officer who seemed to have it all. Jack was the Superintendent's favourite, having been recently promoted to the position Sam had been hoping for, and offered a large bonus to go with it. He had a luxurious house in an affluent area, a smart car and good looks. His life appeared perfect, and he achieved everything effortlessly. Sam often worried Helen would fall for Jack or someone similar, and, even though she had shown no signs of interest, the very idea made him unbearably jealous.

Now he was in his late thirties, Sam's policing career seemed to have hit an all-time low. He knew it wasn't the best paid work in the world, but he tried hard and never seemed to get anywhere. He felt useless and inadequate in comparison to Jack. Most people would be satisfied with a loving wife and happy family, but Sam didn't see things that way.

Walking down the corridor the next morning

towards Interview Room Seventeen, Sam let out a silent groan. The Chief had assigned him to a new case, tackling the recent rise in local shoplifting. This was minor work, unlike the fast-paced jobs at the beginning of his career, working with drug squads, responding to emergency calls and making arrests on the street. It was unlikely he would make any breakthroughs when the important work always went to the younger officers. While they were examining forensic evidence, he was stuck filing paperwork and counting speeding tickets.

Sam followed the passage out through the fire exit into the open air. Rooms Fifteen to Twenty were rarely used, left forgotten in the run-down back building where he had been sent. Sam shivered as he went in. The building was unheated, mainly used for storage, and had an unpleasant smell of damp. He opened the door and the officer who had been watching the suspect handed over the keys and scuttled off.

The room was dingy and uncomfortable, a single light bulb hanging broken and the grimy skylight obscured by years of old bird droppings and dirt. The only furniture was a single table and two chairs. Sam sat down and faced the suspect, a petty criminal arrested on suspicion of fraud and shoplifting: he looked strong and intimidating, with short blond hair, a hard face and dark, knowing eyes. His tattooed wrist was handcuffed to the chair. Despite all his experience, Sam couldn't help feeling slightly unnerved as he placed his file and tape recorder on the grimy table.

'So, Michael Cox,' he began. 'You have been in our custody for nearly a day, yet still refuse to talk to any officers. Is there anything you would like to say?'

Cox, who had been staring at the floor during this introduction, looked up as if noticing Sam for the first time. He said nothing.

'Didn't think so,' Sam continued, rustling his papers. 'I'll start us off then. Firstly, you are suspected of involvement with the notorious shoplifting circle which we believe to be in existence in this town and the surrounding area. You and your deputies recruit local teenagers to do the dirty work, stealing electrical goods, clothing, alcohol and anything else they can get their hands on in the nearby shopping malls and stores. You pay them off cheaply, then sell on the merchandise through illicit business dealings, laundering the proceeds so that you don't leave a trace. We know that you, Mr Cox, are the mastermind behind this successful money-laundering scheme. The thousands made illegally are now mixed in with other currency, and would be impossible for us to track down. Our job is to charge you and put you in prison, so the circle collapses and this never happens again.'

Sam paused, watching Cox's reaction carefully. He

had been hoping to shock him into a confession, but Cox remained unfazed, staring Sam straight in the eyes, still not saying a word.

'I'll ask a few questions now,' Sam continued. 'When did you first engage in dishonest activities relating to shoplifting? I would be interested to know where it started.'

Silence. The only sound was the wind outside and the patter of rain on the skylight.

Sam let out a long sigh, leaning back in his chair. 'Please bear in mind that your silence makes you appear guilty. Sooner or later we will discover some evidence which condemns you, but it would be much easier for everyone if you started talking. A helpful and co-operative subject is much more likely to get off with a shorter sentence.'

Despite his best efforts, Sam was getting nowhere. He was about to give up when Cox leaned forward and clicked off the tape recorder, smiling a little as he did so.

'You seem a decent sort of guy,' Cox grunted gruffly, with an East End accent which had faded over time but was still prominent enough to remind people of his city roots. 'But I sense you're not too happy. The shoes on your feet are muddy and old, your coat is thin and your watch is busted. This interview isn't ideal work for you, it's dull and simple. Probably got a family to support and the pay isn't great. So I'd like to make a proposition.'

Sam was confused. A moment ago he was running the conversation, but now the suspect seemed to be in control. Nevertheless, Cox did sound like he had something interesting to say. It couldn't hurt to listen.

'I'm in a bit of a sticky situation at the moment myself, as you well know,' Cox went on. 'I've made my fortune and was ready to hand over my business for an early retirement. Shame the force had to poke their noses into my finances at such an inconvenient time. The last thing I want is to spend the best years of my life sharing a concrete cell, and I know you could do with some extra money in the bank. How about you discover some breaking evidence that clears me entirely from blame? This case would be dropped, and I'd be ever so grateful. I might just show my thanks by means of a quiet cash delivery from one of my men. Shall we say fifty thousand? On top of that, I'd give you a cut of the profits for the next year. Could be yours easily, no strings attached. What do you say?'

Sam was in shock. He had not been expecting anything like this. Of course he would never agree to accepting bribes from a criminal. The whole thing was ridiculous. He was a policeman, it was completely unethical and against everything he believed in. Imagine what his wife would say if he was caught. Sam had always played it straight, and had no intention of changing.

However, sitting on the crooked chair opposite Cox, Sam began to doubt this approach for the first time in his life. Honesty and integrity had got him nowhere so far, and nobody seemed to be interested in an average, uninteresting man like himself. Fifty thousand pounds was tempting. With that sort of money, he could pay off some of his debts, buy Helen an expensive gift, or maybe even go on a family holiday. There would be more to come after that. Sam could live the high life, just like Jack. Perhaps it was possible. Cox appeared confident, and there couldn't be too much of a risk. The Superintendent wasn't particularly concerned with this case in the first place and Sam was sure he wouldn't notice if it was dropped. A new light had dawned, giving him the confidence to live dangerously. He had made his decision. As he switched the tape recorder back on, Sam nodded at Cox knowingly.

'Interview terminated.'

Three weeks later, it was a very merry Christmas in the Bennet household. Josh tore open a Spider-Man action set, Sophie played with her new dolls and Helen tried on a beautiful pearl necklace.

Sam looked lovingly upon his family as they enjoyed their presents, reflecting on how easily money had transformed him from struggling and jealous to a contented, happy man. He was unaware that it had also made him arrogant and rude. Soon he would be receiving his first monthly payment, one of twelve cuts from Cox's annual profit. He had spent most of the payment reducing their mortgage by half, but made sure there was enough left for a few luxuries. Lunch would be an organic turkey garnished with roast potatoes, vegetables and sausages, followed by a lavish Christmas pudding and chocolate roll for the children. They were having friends over for drinks and mince pies in the evening, and this year it would be the expensive champagne.

Surprisingly, Sam didn't feel guilty or ashamed. In fact, he almost felt proud of himself for managing to pull off such a feat. As he watched the sparkling lights on the Christmas tree, Sam grinned. Life couldn't have been better.

Sam was in a cheerful mood as he walked Daisy along the road one frosty morning in February. Breathing in the deep scent of fir trees, he was humming a tune and admiring the icy landscape when he turned a corner and stopped dead in his tracks. Standing outside his house, leaning on a red BMW, was Michael Cox. This was the last person Sam expected to see. He had not spoken to Cox since their interview in December, and had had no contact with him apart from the collection of a brown paper package on a street corner every four weeks from one of his men. Astounded, Sam sped towards him and hissed, 'What the hell are you doing here? If my wife sees you she'll ask questions and —'

'Steady, steady.' Cox interrupted him with a chuckle. 'Relax. I just wanted to drop this little beauty by to you. Hope you like it.'

Sam's jaw dropped. 'What? Why are you giving me a car?' He knew there must be a catch.

'Just another thank you for saving my back. Oh, and there was something I wanted to ask you. My mate Bill was called into your police station a couple of days ago for possession of drugs. The accusations are completely untrue and I'm sure you would be fine getting him off like you did for me. That's all.'

Sam was speechless. He had naively assumed that his deal with Mike would be a one-off. Now Cox was asking for favours for his friends, and drug offences were a lot more serious than shoplifting. Daisy growled, sensing that this man was dangerous.

'Um, I'm not sure . . .' His voice trailed off.

Cox's expression went sour. 'Look, I trusted you. Do you want in or not?'

Sam had no choice. Reluctantly he replied, 'Yeah, OK. I'll clear your friend, but that's the last thing I'll do. After that I want nothing else to do with you.' He had summoned the courage for these words of defiance, but Cox merely returned his answer with a filthy look.

'You'll regret this, Bennet.' Cox spat on the

ground, scowling, disgusted by Sam's supposed cowardice, and walked off into the haze.

Sitting at his desk several weeks later, Sam's telephone rang.

'Mr Bennet?' came a harsh voice from the receiver.

'Yes?'

It wasn't an agreeable call. 'This is Internal Affairs speaking. We have noticed a drastic change in your lifestyle over the past months, and we find the circumstances suspicious. Copies of your bank statements confirm that you have been cashing in large sums of money from an unknown source. We would like to talk to you as soon as possible.'

Everything unravelled after that phone call. The IA called in friends and colleagues as witnesses, and a mysterious man who seemed to have a wide knowledge of Sam's activities with Michael Cox. Sam was found guilty of corruption and acting as an accomplice to shoplifting and drug dealing, and was sentenced to eight years in prison.

The hardest part was going home to tell Helen. He tried to put everything as mildly as possible, saying he only did what he did to make a better life for her and the children. Unfortunately, she wasn't quite as understanding as he had hoped.

'What on earth possessed you to do such a thing?' she shouted hysterically. 'That's terrible! I can't believe that all the extra money you said was coming from work was really illegal cash from criminal deals! That wealth went to your head: it changed you, Sam. And I never thought you would be the sort to get involved with drugs, I really didn't. I don't know what to say. We had the perfect life before all of this; we weren't the richest people around, but we were happy. Now all of that is gone! What am I going to tell the children?'

Sam's life was collapsing around him, and there was nothing he could do to stop it. He never realised that he had the perfect world, before temptation and greed destroyed it.

The metal handcuffs dug painfully into Sam's wrists as he was led down the corridor to Interview Room Four. This time he was the criminal, not the officer.

'Keep going straight,' said Jack, as he pulled on the cuffs. 'You don't want to take a wrong turn.'

Influence of the Past

Ali Siddiqui

Influence of the Past

The invention glimmered in the otherwise lightless room. I finally allowed my exhausted body to give in to the natural reaction to such hard work and to slump down to the floor of the study. From my watch, I saw it was nearly half past two in the morning, but then my gaze turned to the machine looming over me. It was complete – I'd used particular types of space-energy to make possible something other scientists had been working on for years: time travel.

However, I did not wish to observe the past or future just for interest. I had something much bigger in mind: to alter the past in order to benefit the present. I sat trying to think of a disastrous event in history that could have been less terrible, had I existed at the time. Scanning my head for my achievements in life, I considered how my knowledge of history and my Latin skills could possibly help reduce a past tragedy. Then a thought struck me with such force that my body suddenly rose and headed for the machine in front of me.

My finger became a bullet, hammering in text on the dial found on my machine's inner surface. I typed in my destination, the date and the year: Pompeii, 24th August, AD 79. My aim was to decrease the number of lives lost when Pompeii and the surrounding cities were buried by ash from the eruption of Vesuvius. I shut my eyes to concentrate and stood waiting in the machine. A couple of minutes passed, yet nothing could be heard apart from the faint sound of distant traffic outside.

My eyes opened wide with frustration, but a second later this converted to surprise. There I was, in the midst of ancient Pompeii, with the background noise of commotion in the forums. I was at the back of a building that I could not identify: it seemed to be an unpopular place to visit, which was useful because my machine was less likely to be noticed here. I lay my invention on the ground and buried it in sand to protect it from the earth tremors which I knew would occur before the eruption. Then I turned and looked ahead, to see a dark-coloured mountain standing tall in the distance – Vesuvius. I was suddenly reminded with fierce pressure of the task I'd just set myself. I could not stop a volcanic eruption. But I could warn as many citizens as possible to flee in advance. The sun overhead told me that midday was approaching; I remembered it was afternoon when the fatal eruption had taken place. Time was short.

I found myself running. My goal was to reach any houses containing people, but warning them was easier said than done. An abrupt but violent tremble in the earth made me topple to the ground head-first and roll over, just in time to avoid being hit by part of a stone wall dislodged by the tremor. Immediately I was back on my feet. Through a square window-hole in a house,

I spotted a man eating while reclining on a couch. Suddenly I slowed my pace. My lab coat and buttoned shirt might make the people of ancient Pompeii wary of me. However, I tried my luck and approached the window-hole, managing to use a few Latin words to say, 'Mount Vesuvius will erupt – ash will cover Pompeii and cities near it: you must escape now!'

At this, the man stopped chewing, dropped the meat he was holding into his plate and stared directly at me. Everyone experienced the earth tremors, but I knew some people would think it would pass if they prayed to the gods, and so they would not be too concerned by it. Apparently this was the case with the man I had just spoken to, although I had to bear in mind that my accent would probably be awkward to him, as well as my clothes. Even so, I didn't foresee his response – he called me a 'villainous pest' and hurled his plate at me. Luckily his aim was poor. Well, he'd be sorry in an hour or so. But lingering there much longer was not in my interest – I moved on in my attempt to help the people of ancient Pompeii.

I next tried to warn a few families who either cursed me or tried to get rid of me. But some people seemed to understand, and they packed their belongings and began to escape. Soon crowds of people were running through the ill-fated city.

Another earth tremor pushed me against the wall of a house. The condition of the city was worsening, and, judging by the sun, it seemed afternoon had arrived.

Any minute now Vesuvius would erupt. I decided to caution one more person before I left, but the last man I came to warn became particularly agitated (I must have accidentally disturbed his prayers), rushed through his doorway and started chasing after me.

'So you're the source of this trouble!' His strong Latin voice followed me as I ran amongst a crowd of citizens I had already managed to warn. Then I heard screaming and the sound of pottery shattering as the earth trembled once more.

I didn't stop running, but blocked my ears and turned around briefly to be the only person in modern times to witness the AD 79 eruption of Vesuvius. A sudden burst of flames rose from the volcano's crater, but the terrifying sound, like an enormous bomb exploding, only reached us about three seconds later. An expanding dark-grey cloud then rose and seemed to merge with the flames. I knew the flames would burn elements in the cloud to produce ash, and, later, volcanic pumice stones, which would descend on Pompeii from the moving cloud. Turning round, I was surprised to see that my furious pursuer was still on my tail. As I tried to find my way back to the building where my invention was, I realised it was easy for the man to keep track of me, as with my clothes it was impossible to blend in with the crowd.

An abnormally large lump of sand came into view – my machine. Without looking behind me, I carefully stood my invention up, brushing some sand off it briskly.

It seemed its position and camouflage had worked – it had not been damaged. I had done what I'd set out to do: give people a headstart in fleeing from Vesuvius, thus saving many lives that would otherwise have been lost in AD 79. Although I knew many, like the first man I'd tried to warn, would perish, at least their bones would remain as future evidence of the event.

I slammed in the date and year I had just come from, and typed in the name of my country, city and address on the dial of my machine. Standing in the invention, I closed my eyes and waited as before, but time was running out. I heard a clank of metal, and I realised the pumice stones had started falling. Then footsteps grew closer. My eyes opened to see my pursuer, holding a knife. His will showed in his face. I shut my eyes again and stood helplessly, willing my machine to work. Then his cry of rage grew louder, and I took a peek just in time to see a pumice stone knock the knife out of the man's hand, and another one hit him squarely on the head, knocking him out. Then – blank.

The atmosphere suddenly darkened, and I realised I was back in my study. Although it had been dented in places, the invention had once again worked without my realising. Looking at my watch, I saw that while I travelled to the past, time in the present continued moving as normal: one and a half hours had past since I departed.

Well, I'd been successful in altering the past in a beneficial way; this, if anything, made me more ambitious. Consequently, I found myself searching my mind for an even more significant past event, one that influenced the present far more than the eruption of Vesuvius. Then I remembered how, before World War II, Einstein had written a letter to warn the American president that German scientists were trying, but so far failing, to create an atomic bomb. His letter prompted the US to try to create their own nuclear weapons – and their success led to the loss of hundreds of thousands of lives. I thought how different things would have been if Einstein had not written that letter. I felt that World War II had left a terrible mark on the world, and that, if I could significantly lessen the disaster, it would be the next step in my long-term goal of using my invention to create a perfect world: one where all catastrophes would be reduced to a minimum or become non-existent. I made my decision – to stop Einstein writing that letter to the American president.

For the third time, I tapped the appropriate data on the machine's dial. For the third time, I tried to lose awareness of my surroundings. For the third time, I experienced time travel.

I appeared in America, 1939. My machine was leaning against a tall and dusty bookcase. As I peeked round the corner of the shelves, a white-haired man came into view, walking towards his desk with a pen in his hand. Albert Einstein.

I didn't want to scare the old man, but at least we were both wearing lab coats: I assumed my appearance wouldn't be a problem this time. Just as the man sat down at his desk and began writing the letter, I approached him.

'You wouldn't want to be doing that, sir.'

Einstein's head jolted upwards at once. 'Who . . . who are you?' he croaked.

I tried to look reassuring. 'Please don't worry – I'm a physicist like you.' I told Einstein how I'd managed to manipulate specific forms of space-energy to power a machine to travel through time. When I showed him my invention as proof that I'd arrived from the future, the mood in the room changed dramatically.

'Oh, we must talk – what did you say your name was again? There's so much we could . . .' Einstein began to talk enthusiastically. I would have gladly sat and formally debated with the man who'd influenced the world of physics so greatly, but I was there for a reason.

'I don't mean to interrupt, sir, but I've come because what you are about to do will later cause disaster.' As Einstein fell silent, I continued. 'You must not inform the US government about the German scientists who are trying to create an atomic bomb – that letter will cause the American government to develop nuclear weapons of their own . . .'

Einstein had already grasped the implication, and interrupted knowingly. 'So mass nuclear destruction will happen because of my actions.' His head hung in shame.

I had no choice but to make him feel more guilty. 'And, by 1944, America will have finished building and testing their atomic bombs, and then they will cause more devastation with them, in the war that will begin this year. So, please, you must not let anyone else know of your knowledge, as you will seriously regret it later.' I added that if he didn't write that letter, then the US would not develop their own nuclear weapons, while Germany would continue to fail in their attempts. As long as the letter did not exist and Einstein kept to himself his knowledge of nuclear weapons, atomic bombs would not be created and fewer people would be brutally killed during World War II.

'Well, thank you for that warning,' Einstein said abruptly, and put his pen down. A smile passed across my face. I'd just stopped the creation of nuclear weapons, once again fulfilling my mission. At that moment, however, I spotted a pair of watching eyes at the entrance, and someone stepped into the room.

I saw my feet slowly retreating behind a bookcase and heard them creaking against the wooden floor. My fear numbed me so I felt nothing. I looked back at Einstein, who had only just turned around to see the reason for my sudden hesitation. The man who'd just entered paced forward with a smile of ambition illuminating his face.

'So, Mr Einstein . . . I understand you hold knowledge relevant to the research of my colleagues – relating to nuclear weapons.'

His accent was unmistakably German, and I realised with horror that he must be a spy, and that he had heard me say that Einstein possessed the knowledge that would allow other scientists to produce nuclear weapons. If the spy could get that knowledge from Einstein, the Germans would use atomic bombs, thereby increasing their chance of winning World War II! Horrible imaginings flooded my mind – a world where Nazis ruled, a world scarred deeper by war, a world the furthest it could be from perfect.

The man had his eyes glued on Einstein and he seemed to have forgotten about my presence. 'It's time to talk, Mr Einstein.'

In desperation, I quickly tore a blank page from a book and wrote a message, still hidden by the bookcase.

At that moment, I thought my whole ambition was shattered, as the spy took something out of his pocket. A short pistol glinted in the light of a nearby lamp; I recognised it to be a Luger. Definitely German.

'I said – it's time to talk.' The pistol pointed menacingly at Einstein.

Dropping my piece of paper on the floor, I used my shoe to slide it silently towards Einstein's feet, out of the intruder's sight. The great professor bent his head slightly and seemed to read my message: *Don't panic – I shall reverse time to the moment I appeared behind the bookshelves.*

Einstein nodded very slightly and waited for time to be reversed.

I ran to my machine, dialled in the correct time and place, and, as my eyes shut, heard a loud young

German voice shouting, 'Hey, what?'

The next moment, I was in the same spot, but, looking round the bookshelves, I saw there was only one other person here. A white-haired man walking over to his desk, holding a pen. The invention had worked yet again. Now, as long as I did not interfere, the German spy would not learn of Einstein's knowledge of nuclear weapons.

But, at that moment, I realised that of course my message would no longer exist, and so history would have to go forward as before. Without my warning, Einstein would write his letter to the American president and the atomic bomb would be created and deployed. I quietly sighed as I used my machine to return to my present.

My familiar dark room greeted me as I stepped out of the invention. The sun was now rising. Once again I sank down to the ground from fatigue. Holding my head in my hands, I realised I had learned a lesson over the course of my time travels: perhaps the present is the best possible present. My attempt to change the past nearly made things much worse. I had thought the world could surely be better. But perhaps there is no such thing as a perfect world. Perhaps it's already as good as it can be.

Theoretical Perfection

Cameron Wauchope

Theoretical Perfection

Human beings enjoy routines.

No, not enjoy. Exist upon.

As ants march the same way day after day, or birds migrate to the same location every year, humans have their own individual routines.

We pretend not to have them. We pretend not to want them.

We repeatedly stress how individual we all are, how different from the pack. We say we want spice in our life, spontaneity, something exotic or unusual to keep things interesting.

This is a lie.

Routine gives us security.

Routine gives us the job that pays the bills, the TV shows we watch every night and enjoy, the house we live in and can't quite bring ourselves to leave.

Nostalgia, we call it. Memories.

More lies.

Routine gives us the people we know.

Our parents, there every day after school.

Our friends, there every night in the pub.

Our wife, there every night at home.

All waiting dutifully.

But what does a break from routine give us?

Better yet, consider what a break from routine is.

A break from routine is missing the bus and being late to work.

A break from routine is losing your car keys, house keys, whatever.

A break from routine is your dog being run over by you in your own damn driveway because you were too stupid or rushed to check your rear view.

Man's best friend.

Not anymore.

A break from routine is a plane crash splashed all over the morning papers because all onboard, even the children, died.

Especially the children.

A break from routine is finding out you have cancer, your wife has cancer, your kids have cancer.

It doesn't matter who, it just matters that this is a break from routine.

And that is not what we want.

What we want, what we all want, deep down, must surely be a routine?

And that routine must surely lead, ultimately lead, to perfection.

Perfection.

No noise awoke Leonard Moss (age thirty-four, white, male), or even any action. It was the sun, streaming intensely through his slightly open window. One of those perfect slumbers only concluded when your body is truly ready to awake and meet the world.

Leonard's eyes barely opened, then shut immediately, the bright light blinding in its natural state. He rose out of his bed and approached the window of his third-floor flat, shielding his eyes with his forearm as he did so. He reached out for the blind, then stopped, considered. Leonard opened his eyes and dropped his arm to his side. The miserable weather of the past few days (weeks? Months?) had gone. The sun's rays warmed his skin, but not excessively. They gave comfort and contentment. He stared into the morning sky (clear and blue as far as the eye could see). Leonard considered the view for perhaps the first time. Truly considered.

It struck him this morning, with the sun gently streaming over the trees and buildings in the distance, that the world could be very beautiful sometimes. He conceded that the view was hardly Ayers Rock or Niagara Falls, but for some reason the beauty of the sun over the trees particularly struck him on this day. It was a curious thing to think. Perhaps a result of the warm sun and the pleasant sleep he had recently awoken from, he mused. Or a sudden epiphany, a realisation of the world's true beauty. He shook his head, almost as though awakening for a second time. Hangover, he decided, amused. He smiled to himself as he went to get dressed for work, as the sun continued to shine above the trees and through Leonard's slightly open bedroom window.

Slamming the door carelessly behind him, Leonard (never Lenny, even to his friends) walked at his usual steady pace down the street to work. He passed everything he always did, in the exact same state, sequence and status as always. The pile of newspapers, undelivered, the pet shop, always open, the café on the corner. He continued on his journey, only paying half attention to his surroundings. However, something caught his eye unexpectedly. A white ball gliding gracefully through the air and into the very far corners of a net, a man's hands grasping uselessly at the air just behind the ball's flight. Leonard had stopped outside the television shop, a wall of plasma confronting him.

On every screen was the same thing – one young man, his features lit up in victory. Tim Gayne, hot young striker for Remington Athletic, newly acquired from some commercial brand name division nobody had ever heard of, with the sole job of halting the inevitable, the club's relegation. Leonard stared at the multiple television sets (thirteen? Fourteen? More?) all showing last night's highlights. A life-long Remington supporter, he watched the scene on the screens before him. Several copies of the same upper class voice announcing the same thing in unison drifted through the shop window to Leonard standing on the street outside.

'A late equaliser from Gayne showed Remington still had life left in them, but nobody could have anticipated

*what followed. Gayne followed his first stunning goal with
a second, and finally, in the third minute of extra time, he
made it a hat trick. All this in the teenager's debut game for
Remington and within the space of eight minutes. This will
surely cheer Remington's supporters. They still have a long
way to go to avoid relegation but it has shown that maybe,
just maybe, Remington are not down and out just yet.'*

Leonard stared for some time, even after the
report had moved on to other things. He couldn't
believe it. Remington hadn't won a game that
decisively in a long time. They had barely won a
game this season. Leonard's countenance broke into
a grin, his mind replaying the glorious goals, that had
saved his club's hopes. Today was looking good. He
was still grinning when he entered his cubicle fifteen
minutes later, ready to begin work.

Leonard had set up his employer's IT systems from
scratch. He was retained (and well paid) to monitor
and develop them, and, as the only person who truly
understood their workings, to be there if disaster
struck. He began his working day as he always did by
checking his emails for the usual cries for help. It was
a good way to start his day, as it allowed him time to
get his bearings and settle down as he answered
them before any real work began.

He clicked the *send/receive* button on his desktop. It
chimed back instantly, updating him on his
messages. Leonard wondered what he had received:

emails from desperate colleagues, seeking help? None. Emails from his boss, asking him to work late this Friday? None. Emails from acquaintances, telling him the latest joke downloaded from some bad-taste website? None. Not even any junk mail, telling him he was missing out on the best interest rates since the days of the empire. Nothing, nada, zip. Leonard was amazed. Scratch that, he was bloody well astounded. This was the first time since he had began this job (not this job, any job!) that he could begin without a single email harassing him for something other people believed was within his powers to provide. He was surprised, pleasantly, but surprised nonetheless, and, being a natural pessimist, he was always wary of pleasant surprises. Leonard stood and made his way to his cubicle opening. From here he could see all the way down the corridor to his boss's office. Seeing a light and taking that to mean life was present, he moved swiftly from his cubicle to the office at the end. The class divide in modern society: cubicles to offices. Subtle but substantial, to Leonard at any rate. Reaching the door, he knocked three times briskly and waited. After a pause a shrill voice rang out, perfectly separating the two syllables of the single word.

'En-ter'

Leonard did so.

Susan Ames was not well liked. She was aloof, her employees despised her and even her superiors seemed afraid of her. To reduce the time spent with her, Leonard immediately cut to the chase.

'Miss Ames I was wondering whether . . .'

She, however, was not quite so ready to shorten their conversation.

'Lennie,' – he flinched – 'long time no speak. How's life going for you? It really has been ages, hasn't it?'

Leonard resisted the urge to point out that the only plausible reason you can avoid seeing someone you work for in over a fortnight is because you are deliberately avoiding them. He then surprisingly found himself engaged in the small talk common between 'normal' co-workers. It was fully five minutes before Leonard finally steered the conversation to his problem.

'Susan, I just checked my email and there's nothing new on it. I don't have any new work to do, at least not from my end. Do you have anything you want to give me?'

She hesitated, checking her files, folders, faxes.

'No, I've got everything assigned at the moment. I'm all right, thank you, Lennie.'

'What? Are you sure?'

To say Leonard was surprised would be an understatement. His jaw dropped and, try as he might, he couldn't keep the incredulous tone from his voice.

'Positively, Lennie. Everything is under control – don't fret.'

Leonard was taken aback. Never in his eight (long) years at the company had he ever had no work to do. Never. He didn't know what to do.

'I don't know what to do.'

'Well, obviously there's no work for you for now. I think you'll have to . . .'

Miss Ames hesitated, as though thinking up some terrible punishment for the cardinal sin of Leonard not having any work.

'. . . take the rest of the day off, if you can bear it.'

She was serious, both about the day off and the afterthought of it seeming like a terrible ordeal. Leonard leaped at his chance.

'Why, thank you, thank you, Miss Ames. ('Susan, please.') Thank you. If you need me, ('We won't, Lennie, don't fret.') I'll be on my mobile.'

Leonard left the office. He stood still, contemplating. Then he ran, as fast as he possibly could.

A day off work was cause for celebration in Leonard's book and where better than *The Ass and Fairy Queen*? It was one of those early opening pubs with great food and drink but a ridiculous name (inspired by Shakespeare, no less). Still, the drink was cold and there was plenty of it and that's all that Leonard wanted today. He ordered a pint, watched it arrive, then picked up the glass to drink.

'A toast', he said to himself, 'to Susan Ames.'

He raised the glass to his lips but, before he drank, he thought of something better, more appropriate, to toast. He raised the glass of murky liquid once more, higher, and raised his voice: 'To a perfect day.'

No noise awoke Leonard Moss (still aged thirty-four, still white, still male), or even any action. It was the sun, streaming intensely through his slightly open window. One of those perfect slumbers only concluded when your body is truly ready to awake and meet the world.

He stood and made his way over to the window. The weather forecast had been right. For the past few weeks all Leonard had seen was blue sky and the sun just glistening over the trees visible from his window. Beautiful. Leonard smiled. He'd been doing that a lot lately. He went to get ready for work.

Down the stairs, on to the street and towards his work Leonard went, striding swiftly. He whistled a cheery tune, uncharacteristic of him, but still (he felt at least) appropriate. He continued this melody until a nearby noise overtook it in volume, and proved to be even more welcome to Moss's ears.

' . . . *off Gayne's head and into the back of the net. This gives Remington a three-nil victory away from home and continues their unbeaten record since signing yesterday's man of the match, Tim Gayne.'*

Leonard smiled. Another beautiful day. Another victory for his team. Things were certainly going his way over recent weeks. He continued on to work, smiling profusely at anyone or thing caring to look at him. He didn't care what anyone thought, things were going perfectly. Thinking about it (which he did), he didn't care about anything.

He arrived at work bang on time and immediately caught a lift to his floor. Arriving at it, he strode down the corridor, passing his cubicle without a second glance, and walked straight into Susan ('Please, call me Susie') Ames' office. He didn't even knock.

'Susie, dear, pray tell, do you have anything for me this fine autumn morn?'

Confidence surrounded every word, every syllable, slipping out with every sound he made, every word he uttered. Miss Ames seemed not to care in the least.

'No, I'm dreadfully sorry, Lennie. Seems like it's been a slow few days for you.'

'Weeks, Susie.'

'Has it really been that long? Gracious, where has it all gone to? Well, once again, Lennie, I'm frightfully sorry. I hope you don't mind?'

With any other boss in the world, apologies for not having work to give you would be coated in sarcasm like a chip in ketchup (Leonard's exact thoughts). Not with Susan Ames – she was serious.

'No, it's fine, Susie, honestly, I'll find a way to amuse myself until tomorrow.'

'Really? Oh, Lennie, you have been awfully good about this whole thing.'

While anyone else would fear the dole queue after weeks of not working, Leonard was a realist (but by now a very optimistic one). They couldn't fire him, he was essential. This was a perfect situation, no work, yet still collecting a pay packet. A smile once again played on Leonard's face as he moved towards the office door.

'Well, Susie, you need anything at all, I'm on my mobile. Remember that.'

'I will,' said Miss Ames, the door already shutting as she did so.

Once more, Leonard found himself in *The Ass and Fairy Queen*, just as he had every day of late. It started out as commitment (close enough to get back into work if needed), then convenience (the nearest alcohol serving establishment to his office), and finally it turned into contentment – Leonard enjoyed being there.

He did as he always did. Entered, sat at the table furthest from the door (always empty at this early hour in the morning), removed his phone, keys and change from his pockets, placing them on the table, then rose and stepped over to the long oak bar along one side of the pub. He returned to his table, a pint of beer in one hand, a small glass of whisky in the other. The first time he ordered this, the young girl (eighteen? Nineteen?) behind the bar had raised her eyebrows so far they disappeared behind her fringe, but now she just accepted it as the norm. He always did it. She didn't know Leonard's name, but to her he was just some well-to-do drunk who liked to start early. She didn't much care, he always had the money to pay, and frankly she preferred him to a lot of the less well-dressed alcoholics that frequented the pub at nights. Leonard too had been wary of such an order, not being much of a drinker, but he felt the need to celebrate of late, and there did not seem to be any adverse effects from the drink. He handled it well, never got drunk, and never had a hangover in the mornings. It was perfect. He drank his pint, then his whisky. Always the same order. He did this in approximately twenty minutes and within thirty was back up at the bar. Always the same order.

No noise awoke Leonard Moss, or even any action. It was the sun, streaming intensely through his slightly open window. One of those perfect slumbers only concluded when your body is truly ready to awake and meet the world.

When did the bright light of the sun become so tedious? For the past months (five? Six?) he had been woken like this, always the same, always the same. He rose, so used to the streaming light that he barely noticed it, and, like a drone, walked into his bathroom to get ready for work.

Shirt untucked and unironed, odd socks, he

trudged to work, not strode, not walked, but trudged, taking no notice of anything, the bright blue sky, the melodic bird song, nothing. He stepped slowly past the television shop . . .

'Once again Tim Gayne found himself Remington's hero as he put away four outstanding goals keeping them top of the table for the second month in a row.'

. . . and continued distractedly to work.

Arriving at work, Leonard moved straight to Miss Ames' office. He opened the door slightly, sticking his head through the gap. His body remained outside.

'Anything?'

No words were needed. Susan shook her head. But Leonard had already gone.

At the pub, Leonard ordered a double whisky. He drank it. He ordered another. He drank that. He followed this with more, and more, and more. Nothing happened. He didn't know what he had expected to happen, but he felt no different. Not drunk, not ill, not even remotely drowsy. He had assumed if he could drink enough to make himself completely drunk, drink enough to take him out of his mind, then that could lift this experiment of monotony, this experience of tedium. He no longer felt comfortable in the sun's warm rays which woke him every morning, but contained by them as their heat singed his skin. He no longer enjoyed hearing Remington win their games – they always won. There was no competition, no risk, no danger or threat. This new world Leonard found himself in lacked danger and risk, and he (strangely) found he missed it. He went to work every day, praying that there would be something for him to do, something to take his mind off the routine and his body out of the pub, but there never was. Never. Even if they fired him, it would be a pleasant change, but that didn't happen either.

He came to this pub every day, with its fading wallpaper and ridiculous name, hoping he could drink himself away from this, if only for a few hours. But he never could – nothing worked.

And at the end of the day, when he had consumed so much alcohol he shouldn't even have been able to stand, he calmly stood and wandered home to bed, mental faculties not impaired in the least. 'Why not?' he asked himself every day, after being woken up to the sun and the sky and the birds in the trees. 'Why bloody not?'

Leonard Moss (aged thirty-four, white, male) assumed if he could make himself completely drunk, drink enough to take him out of his mind, then that could lift this experiment of monotony, this experience of tedium. He had assumed wrong. And so he wandered home, to his bed, and the sun, and the sky, and the birds in the trees. Tomorrow was another day. Tomorrow was the same day.

While it may be a lie that we do not want a routine

running our life, it must surely be the best lie in the world.

For we believe it.

We all believe it.

Without question.